VISIT US AT
WWW.ABDOPUB.COM

Published by ABDO & Daughters, an imprint of ABDO Publishing
Company, 4940 Viking Drive, Suite 622, Edina, Minnesota 55435.
Copyright ©2004 by Abdo Consulting Group, Inc. International
copyrights reserved in all countries. No part of this book may be
reproduced in any form without written permission from the publisher.

Printed in the United States.

Edited by: Cory Gunderson
Contributing Editors: Paul Joseph, Chad Morse, Chris Schafer
Graphic Design: Arturo Leyva, David Bullen
Cover Design: Castaneda Dunham, Inc.
Photos: Corbis

Library of Congress Cataloging-in-Publication Data

Rivera, Sheila, 1970-
    The media war / Sheila Rivera.
     p. cm. -- (World in conflict--the Middle East)
    Includes index.
    Summary: Explores the history of television news stations and programs involvement and
influence in times of war, from the Vietnam Conflict to the War on Terrorism.
    Contents: Overview of the media -- The British Broadcasting Corporation-BBC -- Cable
News Network-CNN -- Al-Jazeera -- U.S. national networks -- Media and the public.
    ISBN 1-59197-418-6
     1. Television broadcasting of news. [1. Television broadcasting of news. 2. Mass
media--Influence.] I. Title. II. World in conflict (Edina, Minn.). Middle East.

PN4784.T4R584 2003
0 0.1'95--dc17

2003041845

TABLE OF CONTENTS

One of the ways the media reaches the public is through newspapers.

The TV images of Vietnam were very powerful. Their effect on the public led to the restriction of media coverage in future wars. Since then, more restrictions have been placed on which images journalists can show. Media coverage of Vietnam was criticized for showing the public too much. In another conflict, the media was criticized for showing too little.

During the 1980s and 1990s, the U.S. government learned of famine in Somalia. The U.S. stepped in to help the Somali people. The media also went to Somalia to report about the situation. Some people felt thankful toward the media for increasing awareness of hunger in Somalia. They felt that reporting on the hunger influenced the U.S. government. It caused the government to act on behalf of the Somali people.

Others felt that the media didn't do enough. They criticized the media for not reporting on the Somali famine until after the U.S. government stepped in. By that time, they complained, many Somalis had already died of hunger.

The media was also criticized for only showing one side of the situation in Somalia. Reports focused on U.S. charity. The public did not see what other nations were doing to help. This made it look like the U.S. was the only nation helping.

The media did not describe how food donations from Western nations led to less food production in Somalia. They did not explain how this made Somalis more likely to experience famine. The media reported in a way that made the U.S. look good.

Journalists use Internet and TV to gather and report the news.

During the Gulf War, media reports increased the popularity of U.S. military officers General Colin Powell and General Norman Schwarzkopf. Newspapers printed compelling biographies of the two men. Reporters wrote positive stories about their military actions. They also broadcast news of successful bombing attacks on Iraq. This increased public support for military action in the Persian Gulf.

Secretary of State Colin Powell speaks to journalists.

THE MEDIA WAR

EVOLUTION OF THE MEDIA WAR

Media technology has changed dramatically since the first war reports were published. The earliest war reports appeared in newspapers. Since the invention of radio, television, computers, and satellites, it has been easier and faster for reporters to get their stories to the public.

The first war reporters sprang up during the Civil War. They went to the battlefield with telegraph machines and cameras to capture the action and report back to the people. They used the telegraph machines to tap out messages in Morse Code. Each reporter wanted to be the first to get his story to the newspapers.

Reporting from the battlefield was dangerous then. It continues to be dangerous today. Reporters on the front lines risk being killed or captured by enemy forces. Still they insist on going to the war to get the news.

During World War I, reporters were still using telegraph machines to tap out their stories. They were published in many of the 15,000 newspapers sold throughout the U.S.

Reporters tap out messages in Morse Code from a Civil War battlefield.

In addition to the use of telegraph and photography, a new form of reporting emerged during World War I. The Army Signal Corps and the Navy began filming silent motion pictures. Through the silent films, people were able to see actual war footage. People gathered in movie theatres to see images of war on the big screen. Audio equipment was not available at that time. The films were aired in silence. Much of the war footage was not released until after the war.

By World War II, reporting had extended to radio broadcast. In 1925, nearly 25 percent of Americans had radios in their homes. In 1926, the National Broadcast Company (NBC) became a nationwide radio network.

Americans followed the war by listening to nightly news broadcasts. Reporters traveled with American troops. Radio made live war reports available to the public for the first time. The sounds of fighting gave radio reports an increased feeling of the reality of war. Radio networks also broke into regular programming to broadcast news bulletins. It allowed people to follow the war every step of the way.

By the time the U.S. entered the Vietnam War, television had taken the country by storm. During the height of the war, 100 million Americans had television sets in their homes.

Lightweight audio and video equipment made it easy for reporters to tape news footage from war zones. Television crews traveled freely around Vietnam. Sometimes they traveled with the military. Journalists reported without any restrictions. They showed the brutal reality and violence of the war.

Tapes of war footage were shipped back to the U.S. and ready for television broadcast within 48 hours. People watched news updates daily. CBS and NBC lengthened their nightly news broadcasts from 15 minutes to 30 minutes.

Media technology made great strides by the 1990s. During the Persian Gulf War, American reporters used laptop computers and satellites to send news from Iraq to the U.S. Cable News Network (CNN) broadcast news from Baghdad, Iraq, 24 hours a day. Reporters Peter Arnett, Bernard Shaw, and John Holliman broadcast the beginning of U.S. bombing in Baghdad live on television. Bombs flashed like lighting in the background. The reporters described their feelings of fear and excitement. Americans were able to see the beginning of the war from their living rooms.

Americans appreciated immediate war coverage through live radio and television reports. Many people liked the minute-by-minute reporting. Others criticized the drop in the quality of reporting. They felt that the reporters were not well prepared.

Some argue that the immediacy of satellite journalism allows journalists to report with little or no background information on a situation. They think that without prior research or fact checking, a situation might be misinterpreted. This may lead to false or inaccurate reports.

THE MEDIA WAR

A TV image shows the destruction of Baghdad during the Gulf War.

Live reporting can also be repetitive or unorganized. When two airplanes hit the World Trade Center in New York on September 11, 2001, one reporter said in his live report, "Wow, it looks like either something hit it or something exploded out of it." Another reporter said, "Something has happened to the World Trade Center." He admitted that he was reporting on something that he didn't know much about. The coverage lacked real information and showed the reporters' disorganization.

Advances in technology have made it easy to get information. Technologies such as satellite television and Internet have both pros and cons. People like to have quick access to information. It is difficult to control who can get the information. Sometimes reporters and the government need to prevent certain information from getting into the wrong hands.

Media technology has made great advances since war reporting began. Cameras, TV, and radio brought the reality of war into American homes with vividness that print alone could not do. Satellite television transmission and Internet have allowed the media to bring the news to the world as it unfolds.

Satellites allow reporters to broadcast live from locations around the world.

GOVERNMENT CONTROL OF MEDIA

Most Americans are proud of the many freedoms that their Constitution and laws grant them. The First Amendment to the Bill of Rights guarantees U.S. citizens freedom of speech. This includes freedom of the press.

Many Americans don't realize that reporters and journalists are not always free to broadcast and print any information they choose. Since World War I, the U.S. government has limited the information that the media brings to the public. Governments around the world have controlled their media throughout history.

By the time World War I began, telegraphs and cameras had become popular means of reporting for U.S. journalists. When the U.S. entered the war in 1917, the military was the only source allowed to take photographs from the front lines. Eventually civilian reporters were allowed to take photos. They were expected to give them to the military for approval before publishing them in any newspapers. U.S. military also took control of radio communications.

THE MEDIA WAR

Reporters watch as U.S. forces drop Napalm on a Vietnamese village.

In June of 1917, the U.S. passed the Espionage Act. This act allowed the government to press charges against anyone who published or broadcast any information that was considered disloyal or harmful to the war effort. Many newspapers lost their mailing rights. Some were required to change their stated points of view in order to stay in business.

One year later, the U.S. government amended the Espionage Act. The amendment was called the Sedition Act. This act made it a crime to publish any information or opinion that showed disrespect for the government. This included any negative statements about the Constitution, the flag, or U.S. military uniforms. The government wanted to maintain support for the war. They did this by giving the public only pro-war and pro-American reports. The Sedition Act also prevented spies from printing negative information about the U.S.

Reporting was not restricted during the Vietnam War. American journalists were free to travel through Vietnam. They were able to report freely about what they saw and heard. Reporters, such as Peter Arnett, traveled to the front lines of the fighting. They risked their lives to get the closest coverage of the fighting. Reporters sent videotapes of the war back to the U.S. to be shown on television. There were no restrictions on the ideas or images that were broadcast. At home, people saw the horror of war up close on their TV sets. They saw U.S. troops suffering. Some people were angered by the images they saw.

THE MEDIA WAR

The media brought images of wounded U.S. soldiers back to the U.S. from Vietnam.

Since Vietnam, reporters have been restricted again. The U.S. government tries to prevent journalists from publishing and broadcasting shocking war images. It tries to prevent journalists from taking those kinds of pictures in the first place.

During the Gulf War, the media was not allowed to travel freely in the Gulf region. The U.S. government decided who could film or photograph the military. It also decided when journalists would have access to soldiers, and what kinds of images would be allowed. There were several reasons for this.

First, the government controlled the number of journalists on the battlefield. They did this in order to protect them. War zones are very dangerous places. Many photographers and reporters have been injured or killed while trying to get a news story. If reporters are kept out of danger zones, they are less likely to be harmed.

Second, the government restricted where and when the media had access to the soldiers. They did this in order to protect troops and civilians. During war broadcasts, it was important for reporters not to give away the location of troops. Live television coverage could show troops' location if it was seen in the background. This information could be passed on to enemy soldiers.

A journalist in Saudi Arabia wears a chemical warfare suit during the Gulf War.

If enemy soldiers knew where the troops were, they might be able to attack them. If the enemy knew where troops were coming from, they would also be more likely to leave the area. They could avoid a surprise confrontation.

The Internet has also become a popular means of information gathering and reporting. Most news networks update their Web sites daily. They may update them several times a day.

Internet is easy to access. This has forced the U.S. government to be more aware of the information that is available online. It has had to remove some government documents and information from the Internet. That information was once considered public information. Government officials fear that the information could be used against U.S. citizens by their enemies or by terrorists.

The U.S. government has restricted the media at different times since World War I. Media broadcasting is limited in order to protect the government, the military, and the public. The images that were shown on TV during the Vietnam War made people angry. They did not support their government's decision to fight there. The U.S. government does not want the public to see U.S. soldiers hurt or dying during conflicts. It does not want people to see things that will cause them to lose faith in the government or its actions.

JOURNALISTS AS SPIES

Being a journalist can be dangerous. Many reporters gather news stories in the cities where they live. Some travel all over the world to get the news. Reporters have been known to risk their lives doing their jobs. One reporter who was on the scene when the World Trade Center was attacked explained, "Broadcasting a breaking news story feels like jumping out of a plane and then packing your bag on the way down. It's a bit scary, and, yes, it's exciting."

Journalists often put themselves in danger when they report from the scenes of conflicts. Sometimes the people they are reporting on hurt them. In November 2001, a reporter for National Geographic was hurt in Afghanistan. He was observing a battle between two military groups. A bomb exploded near him. Pieces of shrapnel flew. The reporter's legs were badly cut. He was able to get medical attention and recover from the incident.

In 2001, some journalists in Afghanistan were not so lucky. Three reporters were killed when Taliban forces attacked the group they were traveling with. About a week later, four more journalists were killed by the roadside. More killings followed.

Sometimes journalists put themselves in danger by reporting from places where people do not trust them. In some areas of the world, people do not trust others from different countries. Sometimes people do not trust others who have different beliefs. Often journalists are suspected of being spies for governments or political groups.

Suspicion of journalists is often unfounded. It is not always unreasonable. Governments have disguised spies as journalists. They have done this to gather information about enemies. In some cases, governments have used real journalists as spies. In the 1970s, the U.S. government said that it used more than 50 journalists to gather information. In 1996, the Central Intelligence Agency (CIA) amended an Intelligence Authorization Bill. It gave the government the right to use foreign journalists to gather information. It also allowed U.S. agents to pose as journalists.

The government's history of using journalists as spies has put many journalists at risk. In 2002, a reporter for the Wall Street Journal died doing the job that he loved, gathering the news. His name was Daniel Pearl. Like other journalists, Pearl worked from locations all over the world. He was reporting from Karachi, Pakistan, when he was kidnapped and killed.

Pearl was gathering information about a man named Richard Reid. Reid was a terrorist. He had been arrested for trying to blow

Wall Street Journal reporter Daniel Pearl was accused of spying before he was killed by his kidnappers.

up a U.S. airliner. Pearl learned that Reid had studied under Sheik Mubarik Ali Gilani, a Pakistani. Pearl had arranged to meet someone close to Gilani. He was going to interview him to learn more about Reid. At the time that the two men were supposed to meet, Pearl was kidnapped.

Pearl's kidnappers took him to an unknown location. They insisted that he worked for the CIA. Pearl denied any connection to the government. U.S. government officials communicated with the kidnappers. They told the kidnappers that Pearl was not a government agent. Unfortunately, this was not enough to save him.

Pearl's kidnappers demanded that the U.S. release certain prisoners. They videotaped Pearl making statements about his Jewish ancestry. After about a week, Pearl's kidnappers killed him. They videotaped his murder. It is not clear exactly why they killed him.

The U.S. is not the only nation whose journalists have been harmed. In 2001, Faheem Dasty, an Afghani journalist, was hurt in a suicide attack in Afghanistan. He and two other journalists were going to interview Ahmed Shah Massood. Massood was the military commander for the Northern Alliance. The two reporters with Dasty were only pretending to be journalists. One of them had a bomb attached to his video camera. The bomb exploded. The explosion killed Massood and the man with the camera. Dasty was badly hurt. He was in a coma for several days, and he suffered severe burns on his body.

The Committee to Protect Journalists (CPJ) is an international organization. Its job is to protect journalists. It helps them when they are in trouble. CPJ reported that between 1993 and 2002, 366 journalists were killed around the world. Many of them were threatened. About 23 of those journalists were kidnapped before they were killed. Most of them were murdered.

An astounding number of journalists have had their equipment taken. Many have been held prisoner in other lands. Terry Anderson, a bureau chief for the Associated Press, was held prisoner in Lebanon for seven years. He was held by the Islamic fundamentalist group, Hezbollah. They believed he was a government agent.

General William T. Sherman, a general during the Civil War, once said, "I hate newspapermen. They come into camp and pick up their camp rumors and print them as facts. I regard them as spies, which in truth they are." Whether they are truly spies or not, journalists do face many obstacles in their work. People are not always happy with the information that is reported. They sometimes make it difficult for reporters and journalists to do their jobs. Journalists risk their lives every day to bring the public breaking news.

French journalists report from Afghanistan.

THE MEDIA'S ROLE IN PROPAGANDA

"*Journalists often feel and believe and know that they're being used by one side or the other or both sides. How do they walk a fine line…between being used by, let's say, the Taliban, or, on the other hand, by the Pentagon?"*

-Terence Smith, Media Correspondent and Senior Producer for The NewsHour with Jim Lehrer.

It is important to know that journalists often show only one side of a story. Sometimes the point of view from which a reporter presents a story is his/her personal point of view. Sometimes the newspaper or broadcast network influences the focus of a story. In some countries, the government controls all media. In the news, it is one reporter's word against another. It is sometimes hard to know who is telling the truth.

After the attacks on the U.S. on September 11, 2001, Osama bin Laden appeared on the Arabic TV network, al-Jazeera. He made negative statements about the U.S. In his taped message, bin Laden said that the U.S. was an anti-Islamic country. He said that the U.S. wanted to take over Muslim lands. Bin Laden's statements supported his point of view. They expressed his hatred for the U.S.

Bin Laden spoke deliberately. He expressed ideas that might be believed by people who feared or hated the U.S. The truth is, however, that those statements were false. Bin Laden was using al-Jazeera to gain support from his followers and other Muslims. He wanted them to think like he did. When a person uses the media to influence others to think like they do, this is called propaganda.

In 2003, a voice reported to be bin Laden's made another statement on al-Jazeera. Again, he spoke very clearly. He made more false statements about the U.S. Again, he tried to gain the support of Muslims through his influential speech. He wanted to gain support for his terrorist ideas and actions. U.S. citizens were mad about bin Laden's statements. They felt that he used the TV network to tell lies about the U.S.

The U.S. has used al-Jazeera, too. U.S. government agents have also appeared on al-Jazeera. In late 2001, President Bush's National Security Advisor, Condaleeza Rice, appeared on al-Jazeera. She told Muslims that the U.S. was not against them. She defended U.S. military action in Afghanistan.

The U.S. has also used al-Jazeera to gain information about Osama bin Laden and al-Qaeda. Government officials and weapons experts have examined videotapes bought from al-Jazeera by CNN. The videotapes showed bin Laden and al-Qaeda members training and making weapons. The tapes showed them using various kinds of weapons. Government officials have used the information from the tapes to support their statements about bin Laden and al-Qaeda.

Osama bin Laden speaks on al-Jazeera praising the September 11th terrorist attacks on the U.S.

In 2003, the U.S. was preparing for war against Iraq. A U.S. newspaper quoted retired Marine General Joseph Hoar. He said, "For [Iraqi President] Saddam [Hussein], the goal is to inflict casualties and allow the Arab news networks to broadcast pictures of civilians dying." His statement suggests that Hussein would use the media to show Iraqi people dying. This would make the Iraqi people feel more negative toward the U.S. This could increase Iraqi support for military action against the U.S. This is another example of propaganda.

On February 24, 2003, Dan Rather, a news reporter for Columbia Broadcasting System (CBS), interviewed Saddam Hussein. The two men talked about the possible war between the U.S. and Iraq. Hussein said he hoped to avoid war. He claimed that the weapons he had been ordered to destroy by the United Nations (UN) did not violate the weapons agreement between Iraq and the UN. He also said he would like to have a live debate with U.S. President George W. Bush on TV. Ari Fleischer, a spokesperson for the White House, said that the interview contained "60 minutes of lies, deceptions, and propaganda."

We rely on newspapers, radio, Internet, and TV to give us the news every day. It is important to think about the news that we read, see, and hear. It is important to think about who is reporting it, and what that person's goals might be.

Condaleeza Rice, the National Security Advisor to President George W. Bush

SIGNING OFF

The media has played an important role in wars and conflicts for more than 100 years. Journalists have traveled to the front lines of battles to capture the action and report back to the public. In their quest for war stories, journalists have risked injury, imprisonment, and even death. Even in the face of danger, they feel driven to go to the action.

The methods of news gathering and reporting have changed since the Civil War era. News reporting began with the telegraph. Soon after, films became the rage. Radio and television followed. The sounds of war accompanied World War II images. Soon satellites and computer technology allowed reporters to cover battles live. People no longer had to wait 48 hours to receive TV coverage of conflict, like they did during the Vietnam War.

The government often restricts reporters. During World War I, American journalists were not allowed to print any anti-American ideas. In later conflicts, like the Gulf War, reporters were not even

Satellites and computers have changed the face of the media.

allowed to see any of the fighting up close. The government did not want reporters to show images that might lessen public support for military action.

Individuals and governments often use the media to express a particular point of view. When the media is used to influence people's thoughts it is called propaganda. Propaganda can be useful to gain support for an idea. It can also be used to influence people to oppose an idea. Osama bin Laden used propaganda to gain the support of al-Qaeda members. He was able to influence them to hate the U.S. and other Western nations.

The U.S. and political groups around the world have used journalists as spies. They have used them to gain access to important people and information. This has put many ordinary journalists' lives in danger. Sometimes journalists are suspected of being spies even though they are not. Many reporters have been kidnapped, imprisoned, threatened, and even killed because they were suspected of spying.

Many Americans take the media for granted. They do not think about the danger that reporters sometimes face just to get a news story. They don't think about the possibility that someone put his or her life in danger for the news.

WEB SITES
WWW.ABDOPUB.COM

Would you like to learn more about The Media War? Please visit www.abdopub.com to find up-to-date Web site links about The Media War and the World in Conflict. These links are routinely monitored and updated to provide the most current information available.

During the Gulf War, images of bombings were broadcast on live TV.

TIMELINE

1861-1865 United States Civil War between North and South U.S. forces. War reporters use telegraph machines and cameras to capture the action. News is distributed through newspapers.

1914-1918 World War I. U.S. forces fight with France, Italy, Great Britain, and others against Germany, Austria-Hungary, and Bulgaria. Telegraph machines, cameras, radio, and silent film are used in war reporting. The government takes control of most radio stations. The Army Signal Corps tapes silent films. The Espionage Act and the Sedition Act prevent anyone from publishing any anti-American ideas.

1939-1945 World War II involves the U.S., Germany, the Soviet Union, China, Japan, and others. Reporters begin broadcasting live radio reports from battle zones. War films are now accompanied by sound.

1945-1975 Vietnam War is fought between North and South Vietnamese.

1961 U.S. troops begin fighting on the side of the South Vietnamese. War reporters broadcast war footage on TV. U.S. reporters are free to travel throughout Vietnam and report without any restrictions.

1991 Gulf War. U.S. and allied forces fight Iraq on behalf of Kuwait. Reporters use satellites to broadcast live war reports from Iraq and Saudi Arabia. U.S. government officials prevent reporters from getting close to the fighting. Media in the U.S. encourage support for the war by positively reporting about Generals Powell and Schwarzkopf.

2001 On September 11, terrorists attack the U.S. Reporters use live radio and TV broadcasts to inform the public as the story unfolds. Osama bin Laden uses the al-Jazeera TV network to broadcast propaganda against the U.S.

2003 On February 24, CBS news anchor, Dan Rather, interviews Iraq's President Saddam Hussein in Iraq. It is the first U.S. interview with Hussein in 10 years.

FAST FACTS

- During the Civil War, reporters were not chosen for their reporting ability. They were chosen for their ability to operate a telegraph machine.

- No photographs of dead U.S. soldiers were allowed during the first two years of World War II.

- During the Gulf War, enemy soldiers surrendered to reporters who were covering the situation in Iraq.

- During the Gulf War, U.S. General Norman Schwarzkopf was fondly called "Stormin' Norman" by the media and the public.

- CNN reporter Peter Arnett remained in Baghdad, Iraq, even after all media was told to leave on the second day of U.S. bombing there during the Gulf War. Arnett has reported on 18 wars around the world.

- Al-Jazeera is the only Arab TV network that guarantees freedom of speech.

- Many U.S. viewers of CNN's Gulf War coverage thought the reports were unpatriotic because reporters talked regularly with Iraqi officials.

- During the Gulf war, reporters were divided up into press pools. Only a specified number of reporters were allowed access to soldiers at a time. They were required to pool their information and share it with other media personnel.

- The Arab TV network al-Jazeera was the only television network allowed in Afghanistan during U.S. bombing there in 2001.

- The U.S. said that its bombing of one of al-Jazeera's offices in Kabul, Afghanistan, in 2001 was an accident.

- Daniel Pearl was the tenth reporter to die covering the war on terrorism.

GLOSSARY

Afghanistan: a country in the Middle East.

agent: a government official.

al-Qaeda: a group of Islamic extremists in the Middle East.

Army Signal Corps: the faction of the U.S. Army that is responsible for information management.

Associated Press (AP): a news gathering organization.

audio: used to broadcast sound.

Baghdad: the capital city of Iraq.

Bill of Rights: the first 10 amendments to the U.S. Constitution.

broadcast: to send out a message using radio or TV. Also the information that is sent.

Central Intelligence Agency (CIA): a U.S. government agency that collects and coordinates intelligence activities.

Civil War: war between the North and South U.S. forces which took place from 1861-1865.

civilian: a person who is not a member of the military or police.

coma: a state of deep unconsciousness caused by injury or illness.

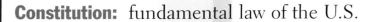

Constitution: fundamental law of the U.S.

correspondent: reporter.

erode: to break down.

footage: film or videotape of an event.

Gulf War: war between the U.S. and allied forces against Iraq in 1991.

Hezbollah: a radical Islamic group based in Lebanon.

Iraq: a country in the Middle East.

Islamic fundamentalist: a Muslim who follows a strict interpretation of the Islamic holy book, the Koran.

Karachi: a city in Pakistan.

kidnap: to take someone illegally.

Lebanon: a country in the Middle East.

maim: to hurt in a way that causes permanent damage to a body part.

Morse Code: a combination of dots and dashes that represent letters of the alphabet.

Muslim: a person who follows the Islamic religion.

network: a chain of TV or radio stations.

Northern Alliance: an assembly of rebel groups that united to fight against Taliban forces.

Pakistan: a country in the Middle East.

Pentagon: the headquarters for the U.S. Department of Defense.

Persian Gulf: a body of water in the Middle East.

satellite: an object sent into the Earth's atmosphere from which television signals are broadcast.

Somalia: a country in eastern Africa.

suicide: to kill oneself intentionally.

Taliban: the Islamic fundamentalist group that ruled parts of Afghanistan from 1996-2001 according to strict Koran interpretation.

technology: use of scientific knowledge to solve problems.

Vietnam: a country in Asia.

Vietnam War: a war between the North and South Vietnamese from 1945-1975. U.S. forces fought on behalf of South Vietnam.

World War I: war fought by the U.S., France, Italy, Great Britain, and others vs. Germany, Austria-Hungary, Turkey, and Bulgaria from 1914-1918.

World War II: war fought from 1939-1945, involving the U.S., France, the Soviet Union, China, and Japan.

INDEX